CALICO ILLUSTRATED CLASSICS

H. G. Wells's

The Invisible Man

ADAPTED BY: Lisa Mullarkey
ILLUSTRATED BY: Eric Scott Fisher

magic
Wagon

Original text by H.G. Wells
Adapted by Lisa Mullarkey
Illustrated by Eric Scott Fisher
Edited by Stephanie Hedlund and Rochelle Baltzer
Cover and interior design by Abbey Fitzgerald

Library of Congress Cataloging-in-Publication Data

Mullarkey, Lisa.
   The invisible man / H.G. Wells ; adapted by Lisa Mullarkey ;
illustrated by Eric Scott Fisher.
      p. cm. -- (Calico illustrated classics)
   ISBN 978-1-61641-103-9
   [1. Science fiction.] I. Fisher, Eric Scott, ill. II. Wells, H. G. (Herbert
George), 1866-1946. Invisible man. III. Title.
   PZ7.M91148In 2011
   [Fic]--dc22
                                                    2010031047

Table of Contents

The Strange Man's Arrival

The stranger arrived early on a wintry February day. He trudged through the snow carrying a small black bag in his gloved hand. The journey from the Bramblehurst railway station to the Coach and Horses Inn in southern England was a long one.

Although he was wrapped up from head to foot, the cold air stung his body. His long black coat and thick gloves did little to protect him from the biting wind. The brim of his hat hid every inch of his face except the shiny tip of his nose.

The snow fell heavily as he staggered into the inn. He appeared more dead than alive as he flung his bag onto the ground.

"A fire!" he cried. "In the name of mercy, a room and a fire!" He stamped and shook the snow off himself.

The innkeeper, Mrs. Hall, greeted him at the bar. After he threw some money at the woman, she showed him to a room upstairs.

Mrs. Hall lit a fire for him in his room. Then she left him alone while she went to prepare him a meal. A guest that found himself in Iping in the dead of winter was a piece of luck. And one who didn't argue at the price of the room? A blessing! Mrs. Hall promised to show herself worthy of his stay.

While the bacon cooked, she returned to the visitor's room with a tablecloth, plates, and glasses. Although the fire raged on, she was surprised to see the man still dressed in wet clothes. He stood with his back to her, staring out the window. His hands were clasped behind him and he seemed lost in thought.

"Can I take your hat and coat, sir? I'll get them dry in the kitchen," Mrs. Hall said.

"No," he said without turning around. He glanced over his shoulder. "I prefer to keep them on."

Only then did Mrs. Hall notice that he wore blue glasses that covered most of his face. His coat collar was turned up and covered his neck.

"Very well," said Mrs. Hall. "As you wish. In a bit, the room will be warmer."

Hearing no reply, Mrs. Hall left the room. Minutes later, she returned with bacon and eggs. "Your lunch is served, sir."

"Thank you," said the man without looking at her.

Mrs. Hall would have liked to ask his name, but he was short with her. *A man with no manners*, she thought.

When Mrs. Hall returned to the kitchen, she heard a *chink, chink, chink*. It was Millie, her helper, stirring the mustard.

"Millie!" Mrs. Hall gasped. "How could I forget the mustard? Surely he'll be looking for

the mustard jar." She quickly filled the mustard pot and carried it upstairs.

Mrs. Hall knocked and opened the door. The visitor moved quickly—so quickly that she only got a glimpse of a white object disappearing behind the desk. It was as if he were picking something up off of the floor.

She placed the mustard jar on the table and noticed the overcoat and hat on a chair in front of the fire. She reached for them. "I suppose I can take these to dry in the kitchen."

"Leave the hat," said a muffled voice. When she looked, he was still crouched behind the desk but had raised his head to speak.

Mrs. Hall was too surprised to speak. The man was holding a white napkin over the bottom portion of his face. It covered his jaw and mouth. But that's not what startled her. It was the fact that his forehead above his blue glasses was covered by a white bandage. Another bandage covered his ears. Not a scrap of his face, except his pink nose, showed.

He wore a dark brown velvet jacket with a high black collar turned up about his neck. His thick black hair, escaping between the crossed bandages, projected in curious curls. Mrs. Hall wasn't prepared to see such an odd sight.

The man remained holding the napkin. She noticed his brown gloved hand. "Leave the hat," he repeated through the napkin.

Her nerves started to recover. She placed the hat by the fire. "I didn't know, sir," she began, "that . . ." She paused a bit embarrassed.

"Thank you," he said quickly. He glanced from her to the door and at her again.

"I'll have them nicely dried," she assured him. As she scooted out of the room, she took one last look at the blue goggles and white bandages before closing the door.

The visitor sat listening to her retreating feet. Finally, he lowered his napkin and resumed eating.

Mrs. Hall returned to the kitchen. "Millie! That poor man. He's had an accident of some sort. Maybe operations. His bandages scared me."

Mrs. Hall unfolded his coat and set it by the fire. "Those goggles! And holding that napkin over his mouth. How odd. Perhaps his mouth was hurt, too."

She thought of the strange man all evening. When she returned to his room to get the dishes, he was sitting in the corner with his back to the window.

"I have some luggage at the station. Can it be brought here now?" he asked.

"Tomorrow, sir. No one can fetch it until then. The roads are steep there and accidents happen. Men have been killed in such weather. The morning light is better."

He started to protest.

"You wouldn't want a man to get hurt, now would you?" she asked. "If you did, it could take him a long time to recover. Don't you agree, sir?"

She continued on, hoping he'd take the bait. "My nephew got hurt and had to have some operations."

"Did he?" said the stranger sounding amused.

"Yes. He did. He had many bandages that needed caring for. Sir, if I may be so bold as to ask—"

He cut her off. "Please get me some matches. My pipe is out."

Mrs. Hall blushed, annoyed. *How could he ask for matches when I'm telling him about my nephew?*

Mrs. Hall left the room and returned to the kitchen. Once or twice she heard him get up and tend to the fire. He often spoke to himself, but she couldn't make out his words.

What a strange visitor, she thought. *What a strange visitor indeed.*

Mr. Henfrey's Suspicions

Mr. Teddy Henfrey, the clock repairman, entered the inn's bar at four o'clock. It was then that Mrs. Hall got an idea.

"Why don't you repair the clock in one of my guest rooms?" she suggested, leading him upstairs.

After knocking, she opened the door to see the stranger sitting by the fire. It appeared he had been sleeping. "Would you mind this man coming to fix the clock?"

The visitor stirred. "Certainly," he said. "You may fix the clock, but I wish to be left alone. And when the clock mending is over, I would like some tea." He sat up a bit straighter. "Any news of my packages?"

"Tomorrow. That's the earliest."

"You are certain?" he asked. "I should explain that I'm a scientist."

"Oh!" said Mrs. Hall. She was impressed. Henfrey was not. He moved about the room and set his tools down.

"My bags contain important instruments I need," said the visitor. "I'm anxious to get them. The reason I came to Iping was to work in solitude. In addition to my work, an accident . . ."

Mrs. Hall shook her head. "I thought so!"

"My eyes are weak and painful. I need to be in darkness for hours at a time. The presence of anyone in my room is stressful for me. I need to work. When I'm not working, I need rest."

Mrs. Hall took a deep breath. "If I may be so bold as to ask—"

"That is all," said the stranger ending the conversation.

Henfrey was slow to fix the clock. He found the stranger curious and hoped to learn more about him.

"Why don't you just go?" said the stranger. "You should be done by now."

Henfrey gathered his tools. He was annoyed. As he trudged through the village snow, he muttered, "Can't a man just look at him? Is he that ugly? Maybe the police are after him! If they wanted to find him, his bandages would hide him well."

As he turned a corner, Henfrey saw Mrs. Hall's husband.

Mr. Hall waved. "How are you, Teddy?"

"You have an odd character at the inn," said Henfrey. He proceeded to give a detailed description of the stranger.

"Looks like a disguise," he said. "I think I'd insist on seeing a man's face if he stayed at my place. But women are trustful. He took a room and didn't even give a name. Ain't right."

"You don't say!" said Mr. Hall.

"I do say," said Henfrey. "He's here by the week so you won't be getting rid of him anytime soon. He's got luggage coming tomorrow.

"My aunt was once swindled by a man coming through town with boxes," Henfrey said. "He sold them to her promising great riches inside. But when she finally opened them, there was nothing but stones inside."

When Mr. Hall voiced his concern to his wife back at the inn, she refused to listen. "Mind your own business," Mrs. Hall said. "You know nothing about him. Don't be listening to what others say."

But Mrs. Hall was worried. She woke up in a sweat at three o'clock in the morning. She had been awakened by a strange dream that huge, white turnip heads with black eyes were chasing her. Being a sensible woman, she rolled over and went back to sleep.

The amount of luggage that arrived the next day was astounding. Besides two great trunks, there were boxes and boxes of books. In addition to the books were a dozen crates and cases carrying objects packed in straw. Most were glass bottles.

The stranger, covered up in a hat, a coat, gloves, and glasses, rushed outside to meet the cart. "Bring the boxes inside. I've been waiting long enough."

As he walked down the trail to the back of the cart, a dog caught sight of him. It growled and barked before nipping at the stranger's hand.

The cart driver snapped his whip. "Lie down!" The dog ignored the command and lunged for the stranger's trousers. A ripping sound could be heard. It was over in a minute.

The cart driver whipped the dog and loaded him in the cart.

The stranger glanced down at his leg and rushed inside.

Mr. Hall was worried. "He was bit on the leg. I better go see if he's alright." He walked inside, up the stairs, and opened the door to the stranger's room.

It was dim inside, which made it difficult to see. When his eyes adjusted, he caught sight of a strange thing. It looked as if the arm of the man's coat was waving at him but without a hand! What seemed like a handless arm and a face with three huge black spots where the nose and eyes should be rushed toward him.

The handless arm reached out and struck Mr. Hall violently in the chest. He was hurled back into the hallway. The door slammed in his face. The lock clicked. It all had happened so fast that Mr. Hall could barely comprehend what had happened.

A few minutes later, Mr. Hall joined the group of people that had formed outside of the inn. Being a simple man, he didn't know exactly what had happened. Therefore, he decided not to bother trying to describe it.

"He just wants his bags," said Mr. Hall. "He ain't hurt."

Seconds later, the dog stood and growled again.

"Come along," said an angry voice in the doorway. Everyone turned to see the stranger with his collar turned up and his hat brim bent down. He had changed clothes.

"I need my belongings. Too much time has been wasted. Bring them upstairs at once."

When the crates were set down in his room, the stranger opened them up at a furious pace. Straw flew everywhere.

When Mrs. Hall took him his dinner, he was so engrossed in his bottles that he didn't notice her come in. When he heard her sweeping up the straw, he quickly put his glasses on.

"I wish you'd knock before entering," he said rudely.

Mrs. Hall sighed. "I did knock. You didn't answer. You can lock the door, you know. Any time."

Mrs. Hall picked up a clump of straw. "This floor is a mess."

"Put it on my bill," said the stranger. "If you must. Put down a shilling. That should be enough."

Satisfied with earning an extra shilling, Mrs. Hall left the room. The man remained locked in his room all evening. Every once in a while, Mrs. Hall heard him shout. Bottles crashed. Books dropped.

She crept to the door to listen. Afraid of getting caught, she reluctantly went away. Although Mrs. Hall secretly shared some of Mr. Henfrey's suspicions, she overlooked them as long as the stranger kept giving her extra shillings.

Dr. Cuss Interviews
the Stranger

The stranger seldom left the house in the next few months. Mr. Hall wanted him to find another inn but Mrs. Hall wouldn't hear of it.

"We never have visitors this time of year," she protested. "Especially ones that give us so many extra shillings. Wait until the artists come during the summer. We'll ask him to leave then."

Although Mrs. Hall rarely had a conversation with the stranger, she observed him each day. Some days he would work and talk to himself every waking moment. Other days she'd hear him pacing the floor and smashing bottles.

He never ventured out at daylight. But when twilight came, he would often go for a walk. His path of choice was the loneliest roads and deserted paths. Those who happened to come upon him would rush home and tell their families of the strange sight they had seen.

He became the topic of conversation in the sleepy town of Iping. Mrs. Hall felt sorry for the man and was certain he suffered great tragedies.

However, most people believed he was a criminal. A criminal who was wrapping himself up so he could hide from the police. This was the story Teddy Henfrey believed and the story he often told.

Some didn't know what to think. No matter what was thought of him, all agreed that they disliked him. He proved irritable and often displayed frantic gestures when spoken to.

One villager had a particular interest in the stranger. The town doctor, Dr. Cuss, wondered, *What was wrong with this man that he required bandages from head to toe?*

When his curiosity got the best of him in May, he set out to pay the stranger a visit.

"I'd like to see your visitor, Mrs. Hall. What's his name?" Cuss said.

"He doesn't like visitors. He wants his privacy." She rubbed her chin. "I didn't quite hear his name when he told me."

The truth was, he never offered a name and she never asked. Standing there with the doctor now and not being able to give a name to the stranger made her feel foolish.

Cuss walked upstairs past Mrs. Hall and knocked on the stranger's door. He opened the door and walked inside.

"Pardon the intrusion," Cuss said.

Mrs. Hall placed her ear to the door but could only hear muffled voices. Suddenly she heard a cry of surprise, a crashing chair, a bark of laughter, and the door swung open.

Dr. Cuss appeared with a look of horror on his face. He rushed past Mrs. Hall. When Mrs. Hall peered inside the room, she saw nothing.

Although she saw nothing, the sound of soft laughter could be heard. Before she had a chance to step inside, the door slammed and the place was quiet again.

Cuss ran straight to the home of Reverend Bunting. He burst into his kitchen and asked, "Am I mad? Do I look insane?"

Reverend Bunting tried to settle Cuss down. "What happened? Start at the beginning."

"I went in to see the stranger at the inn. I pretended to ask for a donation to the nurses' fund. When I opened the door, he shoved his hands into his pockets. He sat in his chair and sniffed a few times. He obviously had a cold.

"As I spoke to him about the fund, I looked around the room. There were bottles and test tubes everywhere. I kept talking, all the while trying to observe every inch of the room.

"'Will you donate?' I asked. He said he'd think about it. Then I asked him if he was working on a secret project. He became quite cross. But I pushed on with my questions.

"He became furious. 'What are you trying to find out?' he demanded. As he rose, one of his papers lifted in the air and carried itself to the fireplace. As he reached for it, his hand shot forward. But you see, that's just it, there wasn't a hand! I don't think there was an arm either. Just a sleeve. An empty sleeve."

Reverend Bunting pulled his chair closer and raised his eyebrows.

"Although surprised, I figured he had a fake arm and had removed it," Cuss continued. "But when I looked again, I realized that there wasn't anything holding up the sleeve. I could see straight in. I tell you, nothing was there.

"'Good God,' I said, staring at his sleeve. The stranger stopped and stared at me with his blue goggles. Then he looked at his sleeve."

"Then what happened?" asked Bunting.

"That's all! He never said a word. He just glared and put his sleeve back into his pocket. I was almost speechless. But my words finally came to me. 'How can you put an empty sleeve like that into your pocket?'

"'An empty sleeve you saw, did you?' he asked.

"'Certainly,' I said.

"Then very quietly, he pulled his sleeve out of his pocket again. He raised it toward me as though he would show me once again. He did it very, very slowly. I looked at it.

"'Well,' I said clearing my throat. 'There's nothing in it!' I had to say something as I was feeling frightened.

"He extended it slowly until the cuff was six inches from my face. I can assure you it's a very odd thing to have an empty sleeve come at you. And then, something—a finger or a thumb—nipped my nose! Tweaked it."

Bunting started to laugh.

"You must believe me," said Dr. Cuss. "There wasn't anything there. You can laugh but I assure you it was real. And terrifying at that.

"I was so startled that I hit his cuff hard and ran out of the room." Cuss took a sip of water. "I tell you it felt exactly like hitting an arm. But that's just it. There wasn't an arm. None at all!"

Reverend Bunting thought it over. He looked wise and grave indeed. "That is the most remarkable story," he said. "A most remarkable story indeed."

CHAPTER
4

An Odd Burglary

A few weeks later, someone robbed the home of Reverend Bunting. Mrs. Bunting woke up suddenly after hearing a door open and close. She shook the reverend and whispered, "Someone is in our house. Listen."

The reverend sat up and rubbed his eyes. Just then, they heard a violent sneeze. The reverend jumped out of bed and grabbed the poker from the fireplace. Cautiously, he went down the stairs. Mrs. Bunting stayed close behind him.

As they approached the study door, they heard a drawer open. Then, the papers rustled. Reverend Bunting could see the desk with its drawer open. As they moved closer, they heard the clink of money. The robber had found their gold!

"No way is anyone stealing our gold!" said Reverend Bunting as he rushed into the room. "Surrender!" Then he stopped, perplexed. The room was empty!

"I can still hear someone," said Mrs. Bunting. "Or something. But I don't see anyone. Or anything." Then she pointed to the candle. "Who lit that?"

Reverend Bunting closed the drawer. "And who took our money?"

As they stood in confusion, they heard another violent sneeze. A minute later, they heard the faint sound of the kitchen door. They rushed in just in time to see the door slowly open and then slam a few seconds later.

The Buntings were terrified. Hours later, they were still frozen with fear in the exact spot. They were too afraid to move or speak.

That very same morning, Mr. and Mrs. Hall awoke early to work down in the cellar. As they made their way downstairs, Mr. Hall was surprised to see the stranger's door open.

When Mr. Hall continued on and saw that the latch on the back door had been pulled back, he became curious. *Did the stranger go for a walk this early in the morning?* He knew he had locked the door before going to bed. Who else could have unlocked it?

He called Mrs. Hall to the stranger's door and knocked lightly. When no reply came, he pushed the door open. The room was empty! Just as he thought it would be!

"George, look on the desk! All the man's bandages are there. His pants, hat, and gloves are here as well. How can he be out and about without his clothes?"

As they started to look around the room, they heard someone sneeze on the staircase. Mrs. Hall peered outside but no one was there.

"Must be my imagination," she said. She walked back into the room and approached the bed. She felt the sheets. "They're cold. He must have been gone at least an hour by now. Where could he have rushed off to so early?"

Then the most extraordinary thing happened. The sheets gathered themselves together and bunched up into a peak. Seconds later, they jumped and danced about the room. Then the stranger's hat hopped off of the bedpost and whirled through the air. It headed straight for Mrs. Hall's face!

At the same time, the sponge from the washstand rose into the air and came rushing toward Mr. Hall. The chair, flinging the stranger's coat onto the floor, turned itself up with its four legs pointing to Mrs. Hall. It took aim and charged her! Gently, but firmly, it pushed up against her back and nudged her out the door.

Mr. Hall chased after the chair, which turned and pushed him out the door. When both Mr. and Mrs. Hall had fallen onto the floor, the door slammed and locked behind them.

"Spirits!" said Mrs. Hall. "He's brought spirits into our inn. Tables and chairs leaping and dancing? We must lock him out. I should have known," she mumbled. "The bandages. The goggles. Never going to church on Sundays. He's put spirits into my good furniture. Perhaps Henfrey's suspicions were correct after all."

Mr. Hall scratched his head. "Let's have some tea and think this over." He led Mrs. Hall down the stairs and into the bar. As the two made some tea to calm their nerves, a voice boomed.

It was the bandaged stranger glaring angrily at them from behind his goggles! He was standing outside his room. "You had no business going into my room. I was promised privacy. Stay out and leave me alone." With that, he slammed the door shut.

"How can that be?" whispered Mr. Hall. "Are my eyes playing tricks on me? No one was in that room a few minutes ago."

Mrs. Hall felt faint. "If your eyes are playing tricks, so are mine." She took a long sip of her tea. "He's the devil, I tell you. The devil in our very inn."

The Bandages Come Off

It was only five-thirty in the morning when the stranger locked himself into his room. He stayed there until mid-afternoon.

At two-thirty, he rang the bell three times to summon Mrs. Hall. She refused to go to her guest. She and Mr. Hall were too busy telling the visitors to the bar what had happened earlier.

When the stranger finally emerged from his room, he found the bar and hallway filled with curious guests. "Mrs. Hall, may I see you please?" he said politely.

Mrs. Hall was waiting for this moment. She had prepared his bill and placed it on a tray. She picked the tray up and walked toward the stranger. "Is it the bill you're wanting, sir?"

"My bill?" he asked. "Why no, you fool. It is my food! Why haven't you given me breakfast? Where's my lunch? A man cannot survive without food."

Mrs. Hall took a deep breath. "Why haven't you paid your bill?"

"I told you three days ago I was waiting for money."

"And I told you two days ago I would wait no more. How can you grumble about waiting for your breakfast when I've been waiting five days for your money?"

The stranger screamed and swore. Some men from the bar rose and approached the stranger. "There's no need for that talk. Pay your bill."

The stranger was angrier than ever. But he forced himself to appear calm. "Look here, my good woman," he began.

"Don't 'good woman' me," said Mrs. Hall.

The stranger reached into his pocket. "I just happen to have the money now."

"I thought you had no money. How is it that you suddenly have it now?" asked Mrs. Hall.

The rest of the men in the bar leaned forward to hear his answer. Word had spread about the robbery at the reverend's house hours ago.

"I found some more."

"You found it?" said Mrs. Hall, thinking of the reverend. "How interesting." She turned to her husband. "He found money."

Mr. Hall suddenly felt brave. "You found it, did you? Ha! By chance did you find it in someone's house this morning?"

The stranger exploded. "You don't understand who I am or what I am!" His voice was so loud, everyone jumped back. Then the stranger started to laugh. "No, none of you understand. I'll show you all! I'll show all of you who I am and what I'm capable of doing."

Stepping toward Mrs. Hall, he put his gloved palm over his face and lifted it away. "Here," he said dropping something into her hand. "A gift for you!"

Mrs. Hall looked into her hand and screamed as she dropped the item onto the floor. "It's his nose. He took his nose off!"

Sure enough, when Mr. Hall rushed toward the stranger, a black cavity was where his nose used to be.

Next, the stranger removed his goggles and everyone at the bar gasped. Soon after, he whisked away his hat and tore at his whiskers and bandages. As they unraveled, women screamed and men shouted.

It was worse than anyone could have imagined. All were prepared for scars but no one was prepared to see nothing. Nothing at all!

Millie was the first to dash for the door. Her screams could be heard all the way down the path. The villagers came to see what was happening. When they got to the door of the inn and looked inside, they saw a headless man.

"It's the devil in disguise," said Mrs. Hall.

"It must be a magician's trick," said Mr. Hall.

The only calm one about was Mr. Jaffers, the town constable. "What's going on? What's the fuss about?"

They all talked of the stranger with no head.

"He must be arrested at once," said Mr. Jaffers. He marched toward the inn. When he looked inside, he saw a headless man holding cheese in one gloved hand and crusty bread in the other.

"That's him!" shouted Mr. Hall. "Arrest him!"

The headless man spoke. "What's the meaning of this?" he backed away and threw off a glove. There was nothing underneath the glove!

Jaffers lunged toward the stranger and grabbed his handless wrist. The other glove flew across the room as Jaffers reached up and put his hands around the invisible neck.

"I have his neck! Grab the feet!" he ordered.

Men rushed forward and reached for the feet. As they did, the stranger's shoes were kicked off and flew across the floor. Despite the absence of shoes, the men held his legs.

"I surrender," said the stranger. "It's no use."

To all that were there, it was the strangest thing to hear a voice come from a mouth they couldn't see.

Jaffers ran his hand over the invisible face.

"Ouch!" said the stranger. "You poked my eye. I can assure you I'm all here even if you can't see me."

Suddenly, the buttons to his coat came undone and the coat came off. Only pants remained on the Invisible Man.

Jaffers walked around the stranger. "This is amazing. But I don't understand."

The villagers started to gather around Jaffers.

"You may not understand, but is that reason to arrest me? What have I done wrong? Is my crime that you cannot see all of me?"

Jaffers said, "Your invisibility is strange but it's not why I'm arresting you. There was a burglary today. Money was stolen. The evidence points to you."

"I can assure you," said the Invisible Man, "that I am innocent. But I will come with you to clear my name."

The body with pants sat down and continued talking. "Clearly, I want to save my name." Then, he jumped up and started to wiggle out of his pants. Soon, one pant leg was dragging on the floor and another was dropping toward the ground.

"Stop him," said Jaffers. "Once those pants are off, we won't be able to see him."

But it was too late. With pants gathered in a heap, the stranger was now completely invisible.

"Where is he?" shouted Mrs. Hall. "Get him!"

What a sight it was to see everyone punching the air.

"Close the door!" shouted Mr. Hall as he fell to the ground. "He's here. He just kicked my shin and pushed me down."

Jaffers made one last reach for the Invisible Man. "I have him! I have—" But he didn't finish. Instead, he was shoved backward and hit his head on the floor.

As everyone stopped and stared, the door opened and a woman standing on the other side was pushed aside. A dog in the street barked into the air and growled. A second later, the dog yelped and ran off as if it had been kicked.

The invisible man escaped. He was free.

Mr. Thomas Marvel

About a mile out of Iping, a tramp sat in a ditch. He wore a furry silk hat that was too big for his head. His fingers fumbled with tying the twine on his faded blue jacket. The twine had long ago replaced the missing brass buttons.

In his hands, he held two pairs of boots. His feet were bare. "Hmmm. Which pair would best suit my feet?"

One pair was too large while the other fit but had flimsy soles. He hated shoes that were too big, but he also didn't like to walk on shoes that wore out quickly. He set them up on a patch of dirt and studied each pair.

"Both are ugly," said a voice behind him.

"And charity boots at that," laughed Thomas Marvel. "I've worn worse. In fact, most times

I've had none to wear." He turned his head around but didn't see anyone there.

"Where are you?" said Marvel. He stood in the trench and twirled in all directions. He looked up in the trees. "I don't see you. Maybe my imagination is playing tricks on me."

"I'm right here. It's not your imagination. Don't be alarmed."

Marvel turned to the voice. "I am alarmed. I hear a voice but I don't see a body to go with it." Marvel rubbed his eyes. "Are you buried?"

No response.

Marvel said, "I could've sworn I heard a voice."

"You did," said the Invisible Man. He took Marvel by the collar and shook him. Marvel's eyes grew wide. "Let me go."

"Don't be foolish," said the Invisible Man. "I'm not your imagination. Would your imagination throw rocks at you?" Seconds later, pebbles were hitting Marvel.

Marvel took off running but tripped over an unseen obstacle and landed on his face. He sat up and cried, "I don't understand! Stones throwing themselves? Something that's not there tripping me?"

"What's not to understand?" said the voice. "I'm an invisible man. I need you to understand that."

"Where are you? I can't see you," said Marvel.

The voice laughed. "Because I'm invisible, you fool. I'm a human being who needs food and drink and clothes for covering. But I am invisible. Invisible to you and to everyone else."

"Let me feel your hand," said Marvel. When the hand reached out to touch him, he jumped back. "You don't have to grab me so hard."

Marvel took his other hand and ran it up the invisible arm that gripped his. He let his hand travel all the way up to the man's face.

"Amazing," Marvel declared. "I can't see you. You're completely invisible except . . ." He bent over toward the voice's stomach. "Have you been eating bread and cheese?"

"Indeed I have," said the voice.

"I don't understand," said Marvel. "How did you do it?"

The Invisible Man ignored the question. "I need your help. Keep in mind that I am picking you to help me. I could have picked anyone, but I chose you. You didn't know I was here next to you. I could have murdered you. But instead, I am asking for your help."

Marvel was confused. "Why do you need my help? What can I do?"

"I want you to get me clothes. I'll need you to do some other things for me, too." Then the voice laughed. "Many, many more things!"

Marvel stood and pointed to the land before them. "I must get going. I need to move on. I'm sure you can find someone else to help you."

The voice screamed. "You don't understand. I'm not asking for help. I'm telling you that I picked you to help me. You have no choice. None at all. If you refuse, then I will kill you. It's quite easy to understand that, isn't it? Or are you a bigger fool than I thought?"

Marvel jumped back but was steadied by the man's invisible hand. "No need to be scared. As long as you do what I say, you'll be safe. I can do great things for you. Think of how powerful an invisible man is." He sneezed. "But if you betray me . . ."

"I won't," said Marvel shuddering. "Just tell me what you need me to do and I'll do it."

Marvel bit his lip and wiped the sweat from his brow. What choice did he have?

Return to the Coach and Horses Inn

It was mid-afternoon when Marvel made his way to Iping. As he passed the villagers gathered on the streets, he overheard them talking of the day's events. Some people spoke of the Invisible Man with fear. Others laughed at the mention of such a man.

Marvel walked straight into the Coach and Horses Inn. Without looking around, he walked past the crowded bar and headed up the steps. Once upstairs, he opened the door to the Invisible Man's room.

Two men were looking through a set of notebooks. They jumped at the sound of the creaking door.

"Who's there?" asked Dr. Cuss. He had been searching through the stranger's belongings with Reverend Bunting. When he saw the tramp, he looked relieved.

"I thought you were the Invisible Man coming back to get us," Cuss said. "Who are you? Are you looking for a drink? That would be down the steps."

Marvel smiled. "Yes, it's a drink I'd be wanting." He lifted his hat, backed out of the room, and gently closed the door behind him. Once outside, he hurried to the window below the room he was just inside.

Up in the room, Cuss and Bunting talked. "These notebooks don't make sense. I can't understand anything in them," said Cuss.

"There are no diagrams or illustrations to help us," said Bunting. "The symbols are confusing. It looks like they're written in a secret code."

"I suspect they're written in a different language," said Cuss. "This here looks like

Greek. And this here," he said pointing to a different book, "looks like it could be . . ."

But the doctor didn't finish his sentence. Something forced his head upon the table. As he tried to lift it, he caught a glimpse of Reverend Bunting in the same position.

"What's going on here?" demanded the reverend.

A voice whispered, "Don't move or I'll murder both of you." It was the Invisible Man!

The men heard a sniff followed by a sneeze. "I'm sorry to handle you so roughly but I have no choice. You have invaded my room. Where are my clothes?" He could feel the men shaking. Neither could speak.

"Look," said the Invisible Man, "I didn't expect to find you here. I came for my books and my clothes. But I can see that you men have my books and my clothes are gone."

He plucked the books out of the men's hands. They watched the books move through the air.

"Since I need clothes for protection, I must ask each of you to give me yours at once."

The reverend found his voice. "Never! I shall never give you the clothes off my back."

At that moment, the reverend's head rose up a bit and then crashed into the table at full force.

"Can't you see you have no choice in the matter?" said the Invisible Man. "Your clothes or your life!"

"It's disgraceful," said Cuss. "But what choice do we have?"

"You're wise to obey me," said the Invisible Man. He allowed them to sit up and undress. He snatched the suspenders from Cuss, wrapped them around his notebooks, and walked to the window. He opened the window and dropped the notebooks to Marvel, who waited below. He then bundled up some clothes and passed them down as well.

Across the road from the inn, Mr. Huxter, a tobacco shop owner, saw the books land in Marvel's hand. "Stop thief!"

Huxter's cries brought everyone out of the Coach and Horses Inn. Everyone except Mrs. Hall, of course. She stayed behind to protect her money in the register. She heard a commotion on the steps. When she looked up, she saw Dr. Cuss and Reverend Bunting half dressed coming down the stairs.

Outside, Mr. Huxter suddenly tripped and fell. Chaos followed! The Invisible Man punched, kicked, and pushed people aside as he made his escape. Everyone panicked and screamed. Women fainted. Brave men suddenly ran away from their loved ones.

Running behind many of them was the Invisible Man. He destroyed anything in his path. He started by breaking every window in the inn. Then, he smashed every glass bottle in Dr. Cuss's office and cut the telegraph wire that led out of Iping.

It was the last time anyone in Iping heard, saw, or felt the Invisible Man again.

CHAPTER
8

Floating Money

Thomas Marvel marched away from Iping carrying the notebooks and a bundle of clothes. His eyes darted all about as he searched for a way to escape the Invisible Man.

"Don't think of trying to escape me," said the voice. "If you try, I will kill you."

Marvel shuddered. "I won't run. I'm here to help you. Ouch! Stop pulling at my shoulder. You gave it quite a bruise."

"I can't trust you," said the Invisible Man. "I think I'll keep my hand on your shoulder so you know I'm always here. Just keep looking after those books, will you? I don't want you running away with them."

"I don't think I have the nerve to help you," said Marvel, shaking.

"You can help and you will help," said the Invisible Man. "It's bad enough that the people of Iping know all about me. You can't escape me and reveal my secrets. To prove how you can and will help me, look at that bank over there."

Marvel looked to the right and saw it.

"Go up the path a way and soon you'll know how you're going to help me. Won't take but a few minutes."

Mr. Marvel sighed and continued walking with heavy burdens on his mind. Suddenly, he saw money floating through the air.

"Take this money and put it in your pocket," the Invisible Man said. "Those poor men had no idea someone was stealing from them. I'm rich! You can be rich too if you help me."

Marvel stuffed the money into his pocket. That night while the Invisible Man rested, Marvel tried to think how he could escape with the money. Anytime he moved, the Invisible Man would remind him that he would kill him if he tried to escape. Marvel felt trapped.

At ten o'clock the next morning, Marvel sat on a bench outside a small inn near Port Stowe. To anyone passing by, he looked worn and tattered. He appeared a bit odd sitting next to a stack of books. After an hour, a man came out of the inn and sat down beside him.

"Pleasant day, isn't it?" asked the man.

"Very pleasant," said Marvel as he fumbled with the coins in his pockets.

"I see you have a pile of books there. You can read all sorts of interesting things in books," said the man. He folded his newspaper in half. "Newspapers, too."

Marvel nodded but didn't speak.

"Take this for instance," said the man. It says in this paper that there's an Invisible Man loose around these parts."

"An Invisible Man!" said Marvel. He laughed. "You don't believe in those types of things, do you, sir?"

"It says here that a doctor and a reverend are witnesses in Iping. They say the Invisible

Man came into an inn wearing bandages and goggles. When he became angry, he took them all off and no one could see him. He hurt a lot of people. It mentions he hurt a police officer, too." He held the paper out for Marvel to see. "It says it all right here. Look for yourself."

"Does it say if he has anyone helping him?" asked Marvel.

"Doesn't mention that. But it does say that he was headed on the road to Port Stowe." The man laughed as he looked around nervously. "He could be right next to us and we wouldn't know it."

The man scratched his head. "It might explain the odd story my friend told me today. Said he saw money floating in the air. I thought he was crazy at the time. But maybe it was the Invisible Man."

Marvel leaned forward and tried to hear if the Invisible Man was still around him. He heard nothing. He didn't see anything moving.

Marvel whispered in the man's ear, "Truth is, I do know something about the Invisible Man. He's— OUCH!" shouted Marvel as he grabbed his jaw. "Ouch!" he shouted even louder as he rubbed his chin.

"Why are you screaming?" asked the man.

"Toothache," said Marvel as he was pushed forward by an invisible hand.

Marvel heard the Invisible Man whisper one word: "Hoax."

"It was all a hoax," said Marvel to the man. "I know the man who started the Invisible Man rumor. Don't believe a word of it."

The man looked Marvel up and down.

"Ouch!" shouted Marvel again as he jumped on one foot. An invisible foot had kicked him in the shin.

"I have a cramp. Must be going," he said.

The man watched as Marvel was quickly pushed and pulled along the road with rough jerks by an invisible hand on his arm.

A Daring Escape

In the early evening, a man sat in his study in a small house overlooking the town of Burdock. Bookshelves and journals filled the room, which had a desk, a chair, and a work area.

The room belonged to Dr. Kemp, a scientist. He was tall and slender and had a mustache. He often looked out the large window in his study to give his eyes a rest from the microscope.

It was on one such break that he looked outside only to see a man running. The small man waved his arms about.

Another fool, thought the doctor. It reminded him of the fools he had met earlier in the day. On his way to town, he passed by several men who spoke about an Invisible Man.

Why all the fuss? he wondered. *As if such a man could exist!*

Kemp was intrigued by the running man. Although he appeared to be running fast, it looked as if his bulging pockets slowed him down. Kemp amused himself for a few minutes before walking away in disgust. *Just another foolish man.*

But the townspeople did not think Marvel was foolish. At first, some laughed at him. But when a child was pushed away from his mother and a dog yelped from an invisible kick, people paid attention.

Panic spread throughout the town. People ran faster with every cry of, "The Invisible Man is here!"

Thomas Marvel refused to look back and ran as fast as he could. He ran straight into the Jolly Cricketers Inn and slammed the door behind him.

"The Invisible Man is here," he gasped. "He's after me and is going to kill me. That's what he said he'd do if I tried to ditch him. For God's sake, help me!"

The barman rushed to the door and bolted the lock. "So those newspaper stories are true?"

A policeman looked at Marvel. "Why is he chasing you? Does it have something to do with those books you're hugging so close?"

Marvel didn't have time to answer. A violent banging shook the door.

"It's him!" shouted Marvel. "He's come to finish me off just like he promised. Don't let him in. Please! Don't let him kill me."

The barman pulled Marvel behind the bar with him. "We'll keep you safe. No one will open that door."

Marvel's face went white. "Do you have other doors? Are they locked? Surely, he'll find a way in and then he'll kill me."

The barman shuddered. "We got all sorts of doors here. Too many to count." He glanced behind him into the kitchen. "The kitchen door is open. Look!"

Marvel didn't have to turn around to know that the Invisible Man was already inside the inn. Marvel was suddenly thrown across the bar by an invisible force.

The policeman took out his gun and shot at the air five times. The large mirror behind the bar cracked into a thousand pieces. The barman and the policeman stood frozen as they watched Marvel being dragged from the bar to the kitchen. Marvel begged for his life.

It only took a second before the officer sprang into action. He lunged forward and screamed, "I got him! I have a hold of something!" The officer and the Invisible Man tumbled to the ground.

This was Marvel's chance to escape!

While the policeman fought with the Invisible Man, Marvel crawled out of the kitchen and grabbed the books. He left through the same door he entered. When he got to the door, he heard a shot and a cry of pain.

Marvel took off. What he didn't know was that a few moments later, the barman and the policeman found themselves alone once again.

As they went in search of the Invisible Man, a plate whizzed by their heads. Five shots later, all was quiet.

"You must have shot him," said the barman. "Grab a lantern and follow me. Let's go outside and see if we can feel around for his body."

Kemp and Griffin
Meet Again

Crack, crack, crack. Dr. Kemp had continued working in his study until he heard the shots. *Who's shooting off a gun in Burdock? What are the fools up to now?*

He went to the window and threw it open. It seemed like a crowd had gathered down the hill by the Jolly Cricketers Inn. Within five minutes, Kemp had shut the window and returned to work.

About an hour later, he heard the doorbell ring. He expected a servant to announce a visitor. When she didn't come, he went to investigate. "Who rang the bell? Was it a letter?"

"No, sir," said the servant. "Just a prankster ringing and running."

Kemp didn't have time for such nonsense. He returned to his study and worked until two in the morning. Finally, he went downstairs to get a drink before turning into bed.

On his way to his room, Kemp noticed a spot on the floor. When he touched it, it was wet and sticky. It had the color of drying blood. Kemp didn't think much of it until he went to open the door to his room. The handle had blood on it as well.

He looked at his own hand to make sure the blood wasn't his. He walked into the room, still confused by what he saw. His eyes fell to his bed. There was blood there as well! His sheets were ripped and torn, too!

"Good heavens, Kemp!" came a booming voice.

Dr. Kemp spun around but saw no one. He heard movement by the washstand but could see nothing.

Surely my mind cannot be playing tricks on me, he thought. He glanced around and quickly shut the door. "I cannot be hearing things. I'm a highly educated man and—"

He gasped! Suddenly, he saw a bloodstained bandage hanging in midair between him and the washstand. He stared at this in amazement. It was a bandage properly tied but an empty one at that. He was about to reach out and touch it when a hand grasped his.

"Kemp!" said the voice as the hand squeezed his hand tighter. Kemp stood there with his mouth open.

"Keep your nerve," said the voice. "I'm an invisible man."

Kemp whispered, "An invisible man? Well I never!"

"I am an invisible man," repeated the voice.

The story Kemp had heard earlier that day raced through his head. "I thought it was all a lie. Have you a bandage on?"

The bandage moved closer to Kemp. "Yes."

Kemp jumped back. "This can't be. It must be a trick." Then he felt a hand grip his shoulder and apply pressure. He wanted to move away but was too scared.

Then the Invisible Man pushed Kemp back onto the bed and the two struggled. When Kemp tried to yell, the Invisible Man stuffed a sheet into his mouth.

"Don't make me hurt you," said the voice. "Steady your nerves."

Kemp tried to kick the Invisible Man but managed to only kick air.

"Steady your nerves and stop resisting me," boomed the voice. "This isn't magic and I am invisible. I need your help. I don't want to hurt you. But if you behave like a lunatic and continue trying to kick me, I'll have to hurt you."

He pulled Kemp off of the bed. "Don't you remember me? I'm Griffin from University College. I've made myself invisible. I'm an ordinary man but an invisible one."

"Griffin?" asked Kemp.

"Griffin," answered the voice. "A year younger than you. Six feet tall. White face. I won a medal for chemistry."

"*Griffin!* What have you done? It's horrible. How on earth . . ."

"It's horrible enough. But I'm wounded and in pain. And I'm tired. I need sleep. Give me food and drink and let me rest here for a bit."

Kemp stared at the bandage as it floated across the room. Then a chair dragged across the floor and came to rest near the bed. It creaked as Kemp watched the seat cushion go down about an inch or so.

Kemp rubbed his eyes. "It's better than a ghost, I suppose."

"You're coming to your senses," said Griffin. "May I have some clothes? I'm cold. And I haven't eaten and I need food and drink."

Kemp walked to his closet and took out a dingy red robe. "Will this do?"

At once, the robe was tugged from his hands. It hung limp for a moment in midair, fluttered about, stood full, and then the buttons were being done. Then the robe sat down.

"How's your wrist?" asked Kemp.

"It's okay. But I suppose I had my first stroke of luck right after I got hurt. Out of all the houses I passed, I found yours to bandage myself in. I wasn't lucky before. There was a fool of a man, Marvel, who tried to steal my money. He succeeded I'm afraid."

Kemp's eyes grew wide. "Is he invisible, too?"

"Oh, no!" said the Invisible Man. "But I'm too tired to tell you my story this evening. It must wait until I'm rested. I feel feverish and haven't slept in days."

"Why don't you rest here?" said Kemp. "Have my room."

"If I sleep, he'll escape with my money. Besides, how can I sleep knowing that men are trying to catch me at this very moment?"

Kemp raised his eyebrows.

"Now I've given you an idea to turn me in," said the Invisible Man. "I cannot trust anyone."

Kemp stood. "You can trust me. I give you my word. I'll tell no one of your secret. You can lock yourself in this room and I promise that you won't be disturbed."

After many yawns, the Invisible Man agreed. "Tomorrow we shall talk about becoming partners. We can do great things together, Kemp. But now, I must sleep or I may die."

"Good night," said Kemp as he reached out and shook an invisible hand. "I give you my word and my word is good."

With those words, Kemp left and locked the door behind him. Then he wondered, *Has the world gone mad or have I?*

CHAPTER 11

The Invisible Man's Tale

Dr. Kemp went downstairs. He lit a gas lamp, pulled out a cigar, and paced the room. *Invisible! Is there such a thing? In the sea there are more things invisible than visible, I suppose. Jellyfish. Microscopic things. But a man?*

His pacing quickened. He noticed the day's papers folded on a table. He glanced at the headline: *Strange Story from Iping.* Kemp read it quickly and saw the name Marvel. Then he caught sight of the *St. James Gazette* lying folded up. He opened the paper and read, *An Entire Village in Sussex Goes Mad.*

"Good heavens!" said Kemp reading the accounts of the events in Iping. *Ran through the streets striking right and left. Mr. Huxter was in great pain. Painful humiliation for the revered. Woman ill with terror. Windows smashed.*

Kemp dropped the paper. He thought, *It's probably all exaggerated. But what about the tramp? Why is he chasing the tramp?*

Dr. Kemp felt uneasy. Kemp so much feared the man upstairs that he didn't sleep that evening. Instead, he paced the house and tried to grasp everything he read, saw, and didn't see.

Kemp gave his servants strict orders to serve breakfast for two in the study but to stay downstairs for the remainder of the day. He too stayed on the bottom floor until the morning papers arrived. It was here that he read the account of what happened at the Jolly Cricketers Inn.

A quote from Marvel was added and more details emerged about his destruction in Iping. But there was no real information on why the Invisible Man chased the tramp.

At once, Kemp sent one of his servants into town to get every paper she could find.

This way, he would know every report on the Invisible Man that was printed.

The more he read, the more he was convinced of two things: Griffin was indeed invisible and he was a man full of rage capable of murder.

Kemp knew what had to be done. He went to a small, cluttered desk in the corner and wrote a note. He tore it up and started another. He reread it, placed it in an envelope, and addressed it to Colonel Adye, Port Burdock. The police chief would know what to do!

As Kemp handed the letter to his housekeeper, he heard a shuffling of feet overhead. That was followed by chairs crashing, glasses smashing, and cries of pain.

Kemp ran upstairs and opened the door. "What's wrong?" he asked the headless robe.

"I forgot about my sore arm and hurt it. I suppose I had a fit of temper."

Kemp started to pick up the shattered glass. "All the world knows about you. It's in every paper. But no one knows that you're here. I don't know what your plans are but I'm here to help you."

The Invisible Man sat on the bed.

"There's breakfast for you waiting," said Kemp, trying to sound calm and relaxed.

The two went down a staircase to the dining room. "Before we do anything else," said Kemp, "I must understand a little more about this invisibility of yours." He looked at Griffin. He was nothing more than a headless, handless dressing gown wiping unseen lips on a napkin.

"It's simple enough," said Griffin. He put the napkin down and leaned his invisible head on an invisible hand. "It seemed wonderful to me before, but now, when I think of what we can do! What we will do! But first, I must explain my story to you. How my invisibility came to be."

Kemp sucked in his breath. He couldn't wait to hear the story.

"I dropped medicine and took up physics at school. Light fascinates me. I was interested in its relationship to solids and liquids. Like the way a piece of glass becomes practically invisible in water when light passes through it."

"I worked for six months and wrote down all my findings in my notebooks—the books Marvel stole from me. I found a general principle of pigments and refractions. A formula that might lead to a possible way to change matter by only changing the color.

"Visibility depends on the action of the visible bodies on light. Either a body absorbs light, or it reflects or refracts or does both. If it neither reflects or refracts nor absorbs the light, it cannot be invisible.

"Think how glass becomes almost invisible in water. Man is even more transparent than glass. Have you already forgotten all you learned at school, Kemp? Just think of all the things that are transparent and seem not to be so."

"Of course," said Kemp excitedly. "Only last night I was thinking of jellyfish!"

"Exactly," said the Invisible Man sounding pleased. "But I kept this work to myself. Oliver, my professor, was a thief of ideas. I couldn't tell him any of this for I feared he'd claim it as his own or want to share the credit. Finally, I asked questions about pigments to fill up certain gaps in my theory. And suddenly, by accident, I made a discovery!"

"Yes?" asked Kemp.

"You know the red coloring matter of blood? It can be made white. Colorless. But it will remain functional."

Kemp couldn't believe what he was hearing.

The Invisible Man rose and began pacing the little study. "I remember the night of my discovery. I worked late into the morning hours. And then it popped into my mind so clearly. One could make an animal—a tissue— transparent. One could make it invisible. All except the pigments.

"I knew to do such a thing would transcend magic. I started to think what this could mean to man. The mystery. Power. Freedom. I saw no drawbacks. None.

"I worked for three years. Three long years on this. Oliver was always asking me what I was working on. When would I publish my findings? And the students! I had enough of their questions as well. Then I discovered that after three years, I would be unable to finish my research. It would be impossible."

"Why?" asked Kemp. "What could have stopped you?"

"Money," said the Invisible Man as he stared out the window.

He turned around quickly. "I had no choice. I robbed an old man. But the money I took from him was not his. So the old man shot himself."

"No!" Kemp whispered.

"Yes," said the Invisible Man slowly. "The old man was my father."

A Man Becomes Invisible

For a moment, Kemp sat in silence. He stared at the back of the headless figure at the window. He thought of the note he sent with his servant and bit his lip. He tried to move the Invisible Man away from the window. "You're tired. Come and sit in my chair."

The robe moved quickly and sat down with a sigh. "I used the money to buy what I needed to achieve my goal. My first experiment happened soon after. I had a bit of white fabric. It was the oddest thing to see it soft and white and then watch it fade and vanish.

"I couldn't believe what I had done. I put my hand in the emptiness and there it was as solid as ever. I felt it awkwardly and threw it on the floor. I had a little trouble finding it again."

"Then, I heard a meow behind me. Turning around, I saw a dirty white cat on the window ledge outside. A thought came into my head. I knew what my next experiment was to be. I opened the window and the cat entered purring. The poor beast was starving. I gave her some milk."

"Did you make the cat invisible, Griffin?" asked Kemp.

"Almost. I mixed the drugs into her food and she ate it. She slept for several hours and while she did, most parts of her slowly faded away. Only the green pigment in her eyes remained. Just two little ghosts of her eyes. When the cat awoke, it made so much noise that the lady from downstairs knocked on my door.

"Did I hear a cat?" she asked as she tried to look past me into the room. "Is it my cat?"

"I told her there was no cat and I politely closed the door. When I turned around, I saw two green eyes jumping out the window. That was the last I saw of the cat."

"You mean to say there's an invisible cat running around?" asked Kemp.

"I suppose so unless it's been killed. It was alive three days later because I saw a mob of people crowded around a corner trying to figure out where the meows were coming from.

"My success set my brain on fire with excitement. I knew I was on the verge of greatness. The prize was within my reach. I was thrilled and danced around my room when another knock came. It was the landlord."

"'What's going on in here? Do you have a cat? Why are you always so secretive?' Question after question! Suddenly, my temper gave way. I told him to get out. He started to protest, but I pushed him to the ground and locked the door. He made a fuss outside and after some time, went away. But I knew he'd be back.

"This brought matters to a crisis. I knew I had to leave the apartment, but I barely had any money left. What choice did I have but to vanish? When I did, I was certain that they'd come snooping around my room.

"The thought of anyone looking through my things and discovering my work made me ill. I had worked too hard to have it ruined. I became angry. I grabbed my three books, the ones the tramp has now, and sent them to the post office. They were sent to a different house on Portland Street."

"When I returned, I mixed the drugs, drank the potion and waited for it to take effect. As I waited, someone pushed a note under my door. It was an eviction notice. I opened the doors to talk to the landlord.

"When he saw me, he gasped. He dropped his candle and ran away down the stairs. I shut the door, locked it, and ran to the mirror."

"I understood his look of terror. My face was white like stone. It was horrible. I had not expected any suffering. But I did suffer

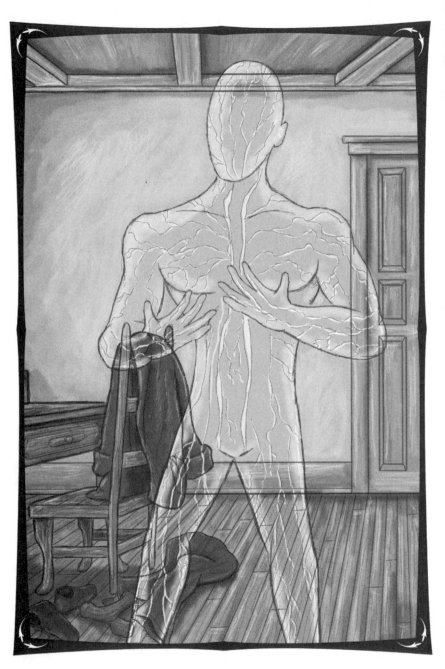

and fainted. My body felt as if it were on fire. I moaned, groaned, and talked in circles throughout the night.

"When I awoke the next morning, the pain was gone. I looked at my hands and saw hands that had become as clouded as glass. I watched them grow clearer and thinner as the day went on. Finally, when I put my hands in front of my face, I could see through them! My eyelids faded. My bones. Arteries. Everything! The little white nerves went last.

"It was hard to get up because I could feel my legs but I couldn't see them. Just then, a loud banging was at my door. It was the landlord and his sons demanding entry.

"I was desperate. I couldn't allow them to see everything in my room. The chemicals. The equipment. So I piled everything into a heap and threw a match upon it and escaped out the window. I burned the entire house down to the ground."

CHAPTER
13

Freedom Brings Problems

"I felt free! I patted a man on his back. I snatched a hat off a woman and took joy at her scream when the hat floated through the air. Startling people was fun! But within minutes, I was in trouble," Griffin continued.

"The air was cold and I shivered and trembled. After all, I was stark naked and the mud on the street was freezing. Foolish as it may seem now, I didn't anticipate that I would still feel all elements of weather.

"Dogs were also an immediate problem. Although they couldn't see me, their sense of smell sniffed me out easily. One dog barked, snarled, and snapped its jaws at me. I was terrified and started to run onto Russell Street.

Luckily for me, a parade was taking place and the dog started chasing the people it could see.

"But the parade brought problems. With so many people on the road, the road became muddier than ever. My footprints started to show. Two boys saw them first and followed me. They chased me down the road a ways. The only way to rid myself of those boys was to find a patch of grass to run through.

"One problem was solved but another met me right away. It started to snow. The snow would lay on me and make a sort of outline. I couldn't have anyone see me. Although I wanted to throw myself at the mercy of a stranger and ask for help. I felt hopeless and didn't know what to do next.

"As luck would have it, I came upon a department store. It sold a little bit of everything. Food, clothes, and whatever I needed to comfort me was available.

"I walked inside and headed straight to the section that sold beds. I rested a bit until the store closed. Once it did, I got to work. I ate until I was full. I picked out fancy trousers, a shirt, an overcoat, and a wide-brimmed hat. I started to feel like a human being again.

"My nose, or lack of, had been a concern. I needed to resemble a man under my bandages. I headed for the toy department and got a plastic nose and a wig.

"I slept well that night. Perhaps too well. I awoke to the sound of men talking. It took me a few second to remember where I was. When I finally remembered, it was too late. The men spotted me and rushed toward me.

"I started to run as I cursed myself for not rising earlier. I raced around a corner and ducked behind a counter. I undressed and watched the men trying to hunt me down. Finally, I left the store the way I had entered it—naked.

"The day was gloomy and I worried about the weather. If snow would land on me and outline by body, then I assumed rain would do the same. I had to sit and think for a bit.

"I didn't know what to do, so I wandered about the town trying to find a way inside a house. All doors were bolted shut. As I started to panic, I saw a small costume shop. I entered it and saw no one. The man must have been in the back and heard me because he shouted, 'Who's there?'

"I stood still as the man came out and poked around. 'Who's there?' he repeated. 'Come out now or I'll shoot.'

"I sneezed, which made him shoot his gun three times. One shot almost hit me! I quickly picked up a stool and hit the man over the head with it. Once he was knocked out, I took money, clothes, and glasses. I tied him up and left him there."

"Did you kill him?"

"I don't think so but if I did, it's no concern of mine. I had to do it."

Kemp raised his voice. "You had to rob and tie up a man in his own house?"

The Invisible Man laughed. "Come, come, Kemp. What was I supposed to do? I needed those items. You would have done the same."

Kemp looked out the window. He knew help would arrive shortly and he had to be careful not to drive Griffin away. "You're right, I suppose. You did have to defend yourself."

"I'm so glad you agree with me, Kemp. We will make a good team."

Kemp bit his lip. "Did you go to Iping next?"

"Yes, and you know the rest of the story. How lucky you are, Kemp, that I'm picking you to help me. Together, we'll . . ."

Kemp interrupted. "I will not harm people. You must know that. I won't attack people."

"I don't want to harm anyone except Thomas Marvel. When I find him, he'll pay for what he's done. I'll kill him." Then the Invisible Man laughed like a madman. "I'll kill anyone and everyone who gets in my way."

A Betrayal

"But now," said Kemp, with a nervous glance out the window, "what are we going to do?" He moved closer to the window and stood in front of it to block the view. "What did you plan to do once you got to Port Burdock?"

"I planned on leaving the country. I wanted to end up in France or Spain. Marvel would have sent my belongings to me. I knew if I stayed here, everyone would be looking for me. It would be impossible to ever live in peace. Now that I met you, my plans have changed. But I still need my books. If I could only get them. Do you know where Marvel is?"

"He's in the town police station," said Kemp. "Locked up, by his own request, in the strongest cell in the place."

"We must get them," said the Invisible Man. "Coming here to your house changes my plans. In spite of all that I lost, all I suffered, I still feel huge possibilities remain. You've told no one that I'm here?"

Kemp hesitated. "No one. That's what I said."

"No one?" insisted Griffin.

"Not a soul," said Kemp as he quickly glanced out the window.

The Invisible Man stood and paced back and forth. "The biggest mistake I made was trying to go this alone. But now I have you. A helper. One who will hide me. One who will give me a place where I can eat and rest. With shelter, food, and warm clothes, a thousand things are possible. We can eavesdrop. Break into houses. It's so hard to catch me. I can easily escape all who try to capture me."

Kemp stiffened. *Was that a noise he heard downstairs?*

The Invisible Man continued. "And it is killing we must do, Kemp."

"Killing we must do?" repeated Kemp. "I'm listening to your plan but I cannot agree with it."

The Invisible Man stopped pacing. "What's that I hear? Do you hear something?"

Kemp spoke fast and loud. "I hear nothing." He tried to keep talking to distract the Invisible Man. "Why must we kill anyone?"

The Invisible Man interrupted Kemp with extended arms. "There are footsteps coming up the stairs," he said in a low voice.

"Nonsense," replied Kemp.

Things happened very fast after that. The Invisible Man walked toward the door, but Kemp tried to stop him.

That's when the Invisible Man knew. "Traitor!" he yelled. "You betrayed me, Kemp."

Kemp rushed to the door and pushed the Invisible Man out of the way. He flung open the door and saw three men approaching.

At the same time, the dressing gown started to unbutton as the Invisible Man undressed.

Kemp rushed out into the hallway and slammed the door behind him. As he went to lock the Invisible Man inside, the key fell to the floor. He tried to reach down for it but as he did, the door flew open. Invisible fingers closed themselves around Kemp's throat. The dressing gown was being tossed about.

Colonel Adye, the chief of police, reached the top step. His face turned white at what he saw. Kemp was on the ground with the life being sucked out of him. His face had gone from pink to white to purple in a matter of seconds. In a flash, the Invisible Man tossed Kemp down the stairs.

Then suddenly, Colonel Adye was struck as a heavy weight, it seemed, jumped on him. As he fell back, invisible feet pounded on his back. Those same two feet ran down the steps and out the front door.

Kemp sat up. "He's gone. It's too late. He's escaped and we will never find him."

CHAPTER 15

An Innocent Victim

"He's mad," said Kemp. "He is pure selfishness. He thinks of no one but himself. He's only concerned with his own safety. Unless we prevent him, he will create panic and kill men. Maybe women and children. I am certain of it. Nothing can stop him."

"He must be caught," said Colonel Adye. "But how?"

Kemp suddenly became full of ideas. "There's no time to waste. We must begin the search at once. Call all of your people in to help. You must prevent him from leaving the area. If he makes it to the countryside, there's nothing we can do. It's there that he'll start his reign of terror."

Colonel Adye nodded and scribbled notes in a small book. "I'll wire for help at once."

"The only thing that will keep him here now are his books," said Kemp. "There's a man at your station that has his books. He's going to try to get them back."

"I know the man," said Adye. "Marvel is his name."

Kemp nodded. "You must prevent him from eating and sleeping. The whole country must be on the lookout for him. Food must be locked up and secured. Every bit so the only way he can get it would be to break into some place. The houses must be locked every second."

Kemp looked up at the sky. "Heaven help us! May we have cold nights and rain. I tell you, Adye. He is a danger. Unless he is captured, he will kill us all one at a time."

"Come with me," said Adye. "We could use your help. You know him better than anyone."

Kemp quickly got his hat and followed Adye out the door.

"Dogs! Get the bloodhounds. They can't see him but they'll smell him. They'll lead us to him. And the road. The roads must be covered with crushed glass. It's cruel, I suppose, but we have no other choice. The man's become inhuman, I tell you. Our time is now."

The Invisible Man seemed to have rushed out of Kemp's house in a fury. A child playing by the gate was picked up and thrown aside. No one knew for sure where the Invisible Man went or what he did. However, we can imagine him running through the hot sun toward the thicket fields in Port Burdock. We can assume that he was horrified by Kemp's betrayal. No one knows for sure what he did between his escape and mid-afternoon.

By two o'clock, the Invisible Man was stuck in town. All trains were alerted to the terror and every single one traveled with locked doors. The cargo trains were suspended so he couldn't hide among them. Within a twenty-mile radius, men walked with dogs, carried clubs, and beat the roads and fields.

Mounted policemen traveled to each cottage warning those inside to lock their doors and stay indoors. Schoolchildren were sent home early for the day. By four o'clock, every person knew that he must keep the Invisible Man from shelter, food, and water.

Before nightfall, a terrible tale was spread from house to house. All whispered of the murder of a peace-loving man, Mr. Wicksteed. He was found in a field and everything pointed to a desperate struggle. His body was found near thicket bushes with an iron rod by his battered head.

Wicksteed was a quiet man on his way home to have his lunch. He must have encountered the Invisible Man, most likely unknowingly. Perhaps the rod was floating through the air and Wicksteed sought to catch it. Maybe he—

No matter. The end result was the same. Mr. Wicksteed was dead and all knew who the murderer was: the Invisible Man.

There's no doubt that the Invisible Man must have known about Kemp's orders and found no way to escape. No train to travel on, no houses to seek shelter, no food or drink available anywhere.

In the evening, the Invisible Man made one last attempt to ignite his reign of terror. He waited until morning to carry out his plan.

A Reign of Terror Begins

Kemp read the letter that was delivered at noon.

You have been clever. Though what you stand to gain by it, I can't imagine. You are against me. For a whole day you have chased me and tried to rob me of food and rest. But I have had food in spite of your attempts. I've had rest.

The game is beginning now. It is time for me to start my reign of terror. Port Burdock is no longer ruled by the queen. It is now ruled by an Invisible Man.

How shall I start my reign? By executing one man today to set an example. The man will be Kemp. He shall face his death today. He may lock himself away, hide, hire guards to protect him, put on armor if he wishes, but death will come to him. Once this letter is received from the postman, the game begins! Help not this man, my people. If you do, you shall die next to him.

When Kemp read the letter, he thought, *It's no hoax. He means it, I'm certain.*

He got up slowly and went to his study. He rang for his housekeeper. "Go around the house at once to be sure all windows and doors are locked."

He closed the shutters of his study himself. From a locked drawer in his bedroom, he withdrew a revolver and put it into the pocket of his coat. He wrote a few notes and instructed his housekeeper to deliver them to Colonel Adye.

"There's no danger," he said. Then he added, "To you."

He finished eating his lunch and thought of his plan. *If I am the bait, so be it.*

He stood at the window looking at the hillside. *Did he really eat and sleep last night?*

His thoughts were disturbed by the ringing of his bell. He peered out the window and saw Adye.

"Your servant's been hurt. The note was wrestled from her hand. He's close about here. Let me in."

Kemp released the chain and Adye entered through as narrow an opening as possible. He stood in the hall waiting for Kemp to rebolt the locks. "The note was snatched out of her hand. Scared her terribly. She's down at the station in hysterics."

"What a fool I was," said Kemp. "I should have known." He led Adye into the study. "Look what I got today. After reading it, I proposed a trap and sent the details to you."

Kemp read the letter. "He'll clear out," said Adye.

"No, he won't," said Kemp. "Griffin is no longer human. He's a wild beast. He'll hunt me down."

A smashing sound came from upstairs. Kemp withdrew his revolver. "It's a window upstairs." As they stood on the stairs, a second smashing of glass could be heard.

When they reached the study, they found two of the three windows shattered. Half the room was littered with shards of glass. Then a crash came from downstairs.

"That fool!" said Kemp. "He's going to smash every window in the house. The shutters are up so the glass with fall to the ground and he'll cut his feet."

"I have an idea," said Adye. "Hand me your revolver. I'll get the bloodhounds and be back soon."

Kemp handed over the revolver but felt uneasy doing so. "I have no other weapon."

Adye lifted his hat. "I'll be back soon. I promise you that. You'll be safe inside."

Another smash could be heard from the back of the house. "Go now," said Kemp, "while we know where he is." They rushed to the door and Adye slipped out. Kemp locked the door quickly once again. Feeling nervous without his revolver, he stood with his back against the door and breathed in deeply.

Once outside, Adye made his way down the steps and to the gate. As he opened the gate, a breeze passed through the grass. Then a voice boomed. "Stop!"

Adye froze but tightened his grip on the gun in his pocket. "What is it?" he asked without turning around. "What do you want?"

"You know what I want. *Who* I want! Go back to the house and force Kemp to open the door for you. For us!"

"You're a fool," said Adye. "Kemp will never open the door for us."

At that moment, Adye felt an arm tighten around his neck and a knee jam into his back as he fell backward. As he fell, he withdrew the revolver and took a wild shot.

In the next moment, a hand struck his mouth and a foot stepped on his chest as the gun was wrestled away. When Adye looked up, all he could see was a revolver floating in the air pointed at his head.

"Get up," laughed the voice. "Get Kemp to open the door."

Adye rose up and repeated, "He won't let me in."

"What a pity then. I have no quarrel with you. But if you can't get us inside, I will kill you. You leave me no other choice."

Adye licked his lips. "If I get him to open the door, promise me you won't rush him. Give him a fair shot."

"I promise you nothing," said the Invisible Man as they climbed the stairs.

Meanwhile, Kemp had hurried upstairs after Adye left and crouched among the broken glass. He watched all the happenings between Adye and the Invisible Man.

A moment later, Adye turned around and started swinging his fists through the air. He reached for the revolver and then fell down. He had been shot!

Adye shook, raised himself on one arm, fell forward, and then lay still.

Kemp stood frozen. In the distance, a ringing and knocking could be heard at the front door. At the same time, pounding could be heard from the kitchen.

Kemp rushed down to look through the window. The Invisible Man had an ax and was plummeting it through the shutters. Kemp backed into the hallway to collect his thoughts. He only had a few minutes before the Invisible Man would be inside.

Just then, the bell to the front door rang again. Kemp rushed over and unlocked the door. It was two police officers who had come looking for Adye.

"The Invisible Man is here! He has an ax and a revolver. He shot Adye!" Kemp gave each man a poker from the fireplace just as a piece of shutter broke free from the wall.

Both men charged toward the ax. One poker stopped the blow and the other knocked the ax out of the Invisible Man's hand. The Invisible Man must have looked through the gap. "Stand back, officers. It's Kemp I want."

"But it's you we want and you we will get," said one of the officers.

The ax suddenly rose in the air and came crashing down on the helmet of the first officer knocking him to the ground.

The second officer waved his poker through the air. Suddenly, a cry could be heard. He had hit the Invisible Man! The officer swung and swung and didn't let up. Finally, no cries could be heard.

The first police officer came to. "Where did he go?" Then he pointed to the open dining room window.

There was no sign of Kemp and no sign of the Invisible Man.

Invisible No More

When Kemp jumped through the dining room window, he headed across the lawn through the asparagus garden. He pounded on the door of his neighbor. Mr. Heelas, a friend of Kemp's, peered through the door.

"The Invisible Man is here! He's after me," said Kemp. "Let me in."

"I'm sorry," said Heelas. "I can't allow you to come in here. I must protect my family."

At that very moment, invisible footprints were retracing Kemp's steps and trampling over what was left of the asparagus patch.

Kemp shook the French doors but realized that it was no use. Heelas wouldn't help him. Kemp ran out the front gate and took off down the hill. As he ran, he saw shimmering shards of glass in the road. He ran over the glass knowing that the Invisible Man would follow his path. He knew what would become of his feet when he did.

As he entered Port Burdock, Kemp heard footsteps behind him. Scores of people ahead of him were standing outside the Jolly Cricketers Inn.

"The Invisible Man is behind me!" he screamed as he ran.

Children and women shrieked and scattered. Men picked up their clubs and charged forth.

"Spread out!" screamed Kemp. "Form a line!"

But he didn't finish his words. A fist knocked into his face and sent him flailing to the ground. Another hand wrapped around his throat and squeezed until Kemp managed to push up. Now the Invisible Man was on the ground, pinned beneath Kemp. "I have his elbows."

"His legs are here. They're secured," cried a man with a shovel.

Many men rushed forth and held the Invisible Man down. There was some savage kicking and cries of "Mercy, mercy" from the Invisible Man, but no one would give any. The cries and kicking finally stopped.

"Stand back," cried Kemp. "He's hurt."

Kemp knelt down and reached his hand out. "His mouth is wet. He's injured."

At this point, all locked doors opened and a huge crowd surrounded Dr. Kemp and the Invisible Man. Kemp passed his hands over the body. "He's not breathing. I can't feel his heart. His side . . ."

A woman screamed. "Look!"

The woman had pointed to an outline of a hand. It was faint at first but grew stronger by the second. At first it was as if the hand was made of a transparent glass. The outline of veins, arteries, and bones could be seen and then they became clouded. Then fully visible again.

Another man shouted, "His feet are showing!"

And so, slowly, the strange change continued. It was like the slow spread of poison. First came the little white nerves, a hazy sketch of a limb, glassy bones, then flesh. Faint at first but solid within a minute. His shoulders and crushed chest were next followed by the rest of the body.

When at last the crowd made way for Kemp to stand, there lay Griffin, naked on the ground. All saw the bruised and broken body of a thirty-year-old man. His hair and beard were white and his eyes were like garnets. Kemp took his jacket off and placed it over his body.

"Cover the face, too," said a man.

Someone from the Jolly Cricketers brought a sheet and covered his face.

Then, Kemp, an old friend from University College, gently lifted Griffin up and carried him into the inn.

Epilogue

So ends the story of the strange and evil experiment of the Invisible Man. If you want to learn more about him, you must go to The Invisible Man Inn near Port Stowe. Talk to the landlord. He is a wealthy innkeeper who no longer wears rags or uses twine to keep his jacket fastened.

If you eat and drink with him, he'll entertain you with stories of his time spent with the Invisible Man. He will laugh as he tells you how he tricked the lawyers who tried to take the money that was found on him in jail.

"They couldn't prove whose money it was. I am blessed."

If you want to see him squirm and stop talking, mention the three notebooks. The notebooks he swears he never had.

But on Sundays, each and every Sunday, when no one is looking, he locks himself into his study and unlocks the bottom desk drawer. He takes out three leather-bound notebooks and places them on the middle of his desk. He sits gloating over the books for a bit. Then, he opens one and starts to work on decoding the strange symbols.

When his eyes hurt, he closes the book and smiles. "Wonderful secrets. Wonderful, wonderful secrets." Then he sighs and thinks, *If only I could unlock these secrets. I wouldn't do what he did. I'd just . . .*

And he thinks of all the possibilities.

No one knows these books are here.

No one will ever know.

No one will ever know until the innkeeper, Thomas Marvel, dies.